NUNGU
and the Elephant

NUNGU
and the Elephant

Written and Illustrated by

Babette Cole

McGRAW-HILL BOOK COMPANY
New York   St. Louis   San Francisco

This is the story of Nungu and the elephant. Nungu lived in a little round hut with a grass roof in a village called Tubu Island, in the middle of Africa. It was a worrying time in Nungu's village, for no rain had fallen for two long, hot years. Nungu knew that unless the rains came soon, the crops, the animals and even the people would begin to die. Madam Hippo knew that without rain the Umvuvu River which flowed around Tubu Island would dry up, leaving her more hot and irritated than she already was.

"It's that Thunder Elephant again, I shouldn't wonder," she grumbled to Nungu. "Most unreliable character if you ask me. Probably gone off on some jaunt with never a thought for others — selfish beast!" Madam Hippo snorted and smacked her youngest son on the bottom.

"What is the Thunder Elephant?" Nungu asked.

"Don't they teach you anything in school?" Madam Hippo grunted crossly, and smacked her youngest son on the bottom again.

Nungu decided to ask his wise grandfather, Ra Dikeladi, about the Thunder Elephant.

Ra Dikeladi was seated under a tree, throwing the bones to discover when it would rain.

"The Thunder Elephant is no ordinary animal," Ra Dikeladi told Nungu. "He lives with the Lightning Bird and the Rainbow Snakes in the land where the two great rivers join. There they make the rain — or that is what people used to believe."

"Don't people believe that any more?" Nungu asked.

Ra Dikeladi, who did believe in magic, looked sad. "Not many people do now. Their heads are filled with modern ideas and they forget the old ways. Perhaps that is why the rains have failed."

After supper Nungu went to bed. He thought about the Thunder Elephant until he fell asleep. He dreamed there was a mighty earthquake. The ground shook and the walls of his little hut creaked.

The creaking was so loud that it woke Nungu up. But it wasn't an earthquake. Through the wall burst a large, gray, wrinkly bottom with a short, bristly tail!

Nungu ran out of the hut as it collapsed. Sitting in the pile of reeds, poles and grass roofing, which seconds before had been a hut, was a large elephant.

"I am extremely sorry," the elephant said in an embarrassed voice. "But I had an itch that just *had* to be scratched."

Nungu stood open-mouthed staring at the enormous creature.

"My name is Jovo." The elephant blushed. "I felt so neglected and unwanted at home that I ran away. I have wandered all over the forest for months and nobody wants me. May I stay here please?"

And that is how the elephant came to Tubu Island. At first the people thought that having an elephant would be a good omen (for elephants are usually shy and keep away from villages). But they soon changed their minds and realized why Jovo had been such an unwelcome visitor elsewhere in the forest.

Jovo was remarkably clumsy for an elephant. Every time he had an itch he scratched it on a hut. This cured the itch — but demolished the hut!

Every time he went for a stroll, he squashed everything in his path. He even got his foot stuck in a cooking pot. Soon the village looked as if it really had been hit by an earthquake.

Jovo spent most of the day rubbing his head on the Oro tree by Nungu's new hut, so that the heavy pods fell off. These sausage-shaped pods were his favorite food. This made Masheety, Nungu's lazy donkey, very cross because Oro pods were his favorite food too.

At night Jovo liked to sleep close to the cooking fires. But one night he rolled right on top of the warm embers. He charged around the village shouting, "FIRE! FIRE!" Everyone was very alarmed and ran about with calabashes of water until they discovered that there was no fire — just an elephant with a singed belly button.

The people of Nungu's village asked Jovo to leave . . . but he stuck his feet in his ears. They tried to push him out . . . but he sat down and pretended to be asleep. They threw sticks at him . . . but that did not work either.

When they had gone away Jovo opened one eye and looked at Nungu.

"Nobody loves me," he moaned. "Nobody needs me. Nobody even believes in me any more! And after all the hundreds of years I've spent making rain. It's not fair that nobody believes in me!"

"Believes in you?" Nungu said, puzzled. "Jovo . . . you are the Thunder Elephant! You make the rain!"

"Not any more I don't," Jovo said crossly. "I'm never going to make rain again . . . EVER!" And he clanked back to the Oro tree with the cooking pot still on his foot — straight through Nungu's mother's washing line!

Nungu told Madam Hippo that Jovo was the Thunder Elephant. She was astonished.

"Nungu, you are very clever, you must make Jovo go home," Madam Hippo said, and her three sons agreed.

"It just happens that I have a plan," said Nungu. And he whispered in Madam Hippo's little ear. Gradually a wide grin spread across her face.

Nungu went back to the village and marched up to Jovo. "I challenge you to a tug of war," he said. "If you can pull me out of the river, you can stay here. If I pull you into the river, you must go home to the Lightning Bird and the Rainbow Snakes and make rain."

"Ha, ha, ha, hee, hee, ho, ho!" laughed Jovo, rolling about on the grass holding his sides. "YOU pull ME into the river! Go and fetch a rope . . . heee, hee . . . and I'll show you."

Nungu ran to Ra Dikeladi's hut. "Grandfather, please come with me and bring your strongest rope. I'm going to have a tug of war with the elephant."

Ra Dikeladi, who never underestimated Nungu, found a rope made of tree bark. They took it down to the river where Jovo was waiting and still laughing.

"Now," said Nungu, "take this end of the rope. I will wade to the papyrus grass with the other end. When Ra Dikeladi says 'Go', start pulling."

Nungu waded out to the floating platform of papyrus grass. He climbed onto it and dangled his end of the rope in the water. Madam Hippo was waiting under the water with her three sons. She seized the rope and gave a little pull to tell Nungu she was ready.

"Go!" shouted Ra Dikeladi, and the tug of war began.

Jovo pulled. Nungu pretended to pull. Under the water, Madam Hippo and her three sons pulled and pulled and pulled.

SPLOSH! Jovo went head first into the river. He came up covered with mud and little green frogs.

Nungu cheered. Ra Dikeladi chuckled. Under the water, the hippos laughed and slapped each other on the back.

Nungu brushed the frogs out of Jovo's ears.

"Time I was leaving," said the elephant with a sigh.

Nungu decided to go with Jovo to the land where the two rivers join. He wanted to be sure that the elephant arrived safely. He also wanted to make Jovo feel loved and needed.

He told his grandfather all about Jovo. Ra Dikeladi was worried about Nungu meeting the Lightning Bird.

"He is very fierce," Ra Dikeladi said, "and may attack a stranger." He went to the special tree where his medicines hung and took down a beautiful, bead-covered pipe. "This is the Flute of Heaven," Ra Dikeladi said. "If the Lightning Bird does attack you, blow this flute. Then the bird will grow quiet and do you no harm."

So Nungu took the magic flute and set off with Jovo and Masheety for the land where the two rivers join. Masheety was so slow that Jovo told Nungu and the donkey to climb on his broad back. Soon Masheety was fast asleep.

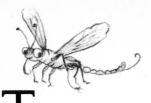

They followed the Umvuvu River for many miles until they met a herd of zebras.

"Where are you going?" the zebras asked.

"This is the mighty Thunder Elephant. He makes the rain," Nungu said in a proud voice. "We are taking him home."

"The Thunder Elephant!" the zebras said. "He is very important. We will go with you."

Along the path, they met the giraffes, who peeped out of the treetops and said, "That must be the mighty Thunder Elephant. We'd like to come too."

Jovo saw that lots of people still believed in him, and needed him. He marched along feeling very pleased with himself.

The rhinos soon joined in, followed by the lions, the buffaloes, the warthogs and every creature down to the last mosquito. They all wanted to escort the Thunder Elephant home.

The procession wound its way along the river, through the forest, over the flood plains, out into the savannah and away towards the mountains to the land of the Lightning Bird and the Rainbow Snakes.

Here the great Umvuvu River joined the great Zimbanzi River. They fell away together in a beautiful waterfall that roared like a million lions. Dancing over the water were seven lovely rainbows.

Nungu and all the animals stood gazing at the waterfall. Then . . . up in the sky there was a terrible flash! The clouds parted and down came the awful Lightning Bird. His long, sword-like beak gleamed and flashed as he made straight for Nungu.

Nungu remembered his grandfather's flute. "Psee . . Psee . . Psee," he blew.

The bird slowed, turned, and with a flutter of feathers settled on a rock.

"Where have you been?" the Lightning Bird said crossly to the elephant. "Rangi, Odingi, Gwaunu, Bundi, Yahwe, Iandi, Voopoo . . . HE'S BACK!"

The rainbows stopped dancing and settled on the grass. Nungu could see that they were not rainbows at all, but seven shiny snakes.

The Rainbow Snakes smiled and wriggled. "Welcome home, Jovo," they said. "We have missssed you sssso."

The Thunder Elephant smiled. "I would not have come home at all if it weren't for Nungu."

"Yes, yes," said the Lightning Bird hurriedly. "This is all very nice, but there's no time to lose. Get up that mountain and make some thunder!"

"Thank you, Nungu," said Jovo. "I'll come and visit you in the dry season when I have my holidays."

"There will always be Oro pods for you," Nungu said, laughing, "but you'll have to bring your own back-scratcher!"

The Rainbow Snakes flew over the waterfall to make a bridge for Jovo to walk on. The Lightning Bird flapped behind, muttering, "We're late . . . we're so late!"

As soon as they had reached the mountain and the Rainbow Snakes had rolled up behind him, Jovo roared a wonderful clap of thunder.

Down came the rain in torrents. Nungu and the animals danced and shouted, "Thank you, Jovo. Thank you. Thank you."

Masheety, who had slept through the whole thing, woke up because he was getting wet and wanted to go home. So the long line of animals made its way back to Tubu Island.

Now the rain had come, the people could start plowing and planting their crops again. When they heard who Jovo really was, they remembered the old belief about the Thunder Elephant, the Lightning Bird and the Rainbow Snakes.

Nobody really knew how Jovo had been persuaded to go home . . . and it is still a secret. Only Madam Hippo knows . . . and her three sons . . . and Ra Dikeladi . . . and of course, clever little Nungu.

astin powers on
tv. are chonilies

riht nore

They all have a good chuckle about it!

Copyright © 1980 by Babette Cole. All rights reserved.

First published in Great Britain in 1980 by
Macdonald General Books.
Macdonald and Jane's Publishers Limited,
Paulton House, 8 Shepherdess Walk, London N1 7LW.

First published and distributed in the United
States of America in 1980 by McGraw-Hill Book Company,
1221 Avenue of the Americas, New York, N.Y. 10020.

Printed and bound in Hong Kong by
Leefung-Asco Printers Ltd

123456789   876543210

Library of Congress Cataloging in
Publication Data

Cole, Babette.
  Nungu and the elephant.

  SUMMARY: A young African boy living in
an area that hasn't had rain for two years
befriends a clumsy elephant that wanders
into the village and discovers that he is one
of the three animals responsible for
making rain.
  [1. Rain and rainfall – Fiction.
2. Africa – Fiction]
I. Title.
PZ7.C6734Nr [E] 79-27777
ISBN 0-07-011696-2